# ON THE SUBJECT OF TROLLS

First published in Great Britain in 2019
**ISBN 9781085814294**

Written by Benjamin T. Milnes
from November 2017 to July 2019

Copyright © Benjamin T. Milnes

All rights reserved; no part of this publication may be reproduced or transmitted by any means: electronic, mechanical, or otherwise, without the written permission of the author.

Discover more from Benjamin T. Milnes at
www.benjamintmilnes.com

# ON THE SUBJECT OF TROLLS

AS TOLD BY
AELFRAED OF CIRNECEASTER

TRANSCRIBED BY
BENJAMIN T. MILNES

# THROCH
# THE CUNNING

There was once a troll, whose name was Throch. Like all trolls, he was not beautiful. The skin of his face was ashen, and his eyes and mouth were prunish. His thighs were mottled yellow with clumped fat, and his gnarled hands dripped with black snot. Throch, however, thought himself truly stunning to look upon. He was bald – like all trolls – but each day smeared a sod of piss-stained straw on his head. He also had a taste for costly and garish clothing and jewellery, which he acquired from aethelings and thanes he met upon the road.

I would not say that Throch was *wise*, but he was *cunning* – far more so than most trolls. He had a knowledge of what he wanted and had at some point stumbled upon a way of getting it. You see, Throch did not acquire these gifts from the aethelings and thanes he met by threatening them, in the way that the common troll might. No, Throch had a way with words. After speaking with the aethelings, reeves, and thanes for a few minutes, they gladly gave him an ermine coat or a gold ring or a bottle of perfume.

The tale I will tell you happened in the eighteenth year of the reign of King Aethelraed. Aethelraed was a truly great king. His grandfather, King Eadric, had usurped the throne from King Cyneric, and within two years after being crowned had killed any reeve or thane who so much as whispered malcontent. His son, and Aethelraed's father, King Eadthryth, had continued to remove any disloyal lords, and as such when Aethelraed came to the throne at twenty-four years old, he was completely unopposed in the royal court.

Gruesome though his father and grandfather were, the peaceful upbringing that the young Aethelraed had gave him much time for reading the great histories of the land and disquisitions on mathematics and medicine, and so by the time that his father died, he was knowledgeable of the kings of the past – their rulings, their mistakes – and a great many other things. Thus, Aethelraed quickly showed himself to be a wise king. In the first five years of his reign, he commissioned the writing of a handbook, describing the latest innovations in agriculture, which was then copied and distributed to all of the towns in the kingdom. He also designed a new type of device for foretelling the seasons.

Aethelraed also believed that any man or woman, be they noble or common, should be able to speak their mind on any matter without persecution. He believed that good ideas could come from anyone – not just those of nobility – thus he wanted to hear what everyone had to say. Two years into his reign he decreed that no-one may strike or kill another just because of something that they said. And by the time of this story, the people of the kingdom had adjusted to this.

And so Aethelraed became known as a wise king. His father and grandfather had ruled through strength, and so no-one had dared to oppose them, but with Aethelraed, who ruled through wisdom, no-one wanted to oppose him.

But though Aethelraed was wise, he was not cunning, as Throch was. And this, it seemed, was his undoing when it came to the troll.

No-one knows what Throch did for the first thirty years of his miserable life. It is assumed that he did what most trolls do: hassle men and women (though mostly women – particularly those who did not wear what he wanted them to wear) who travelled from town to town along muddy roads. He stole food, and sat in sodden earth by the roadside, tearing chunks off it with his yellow teeth.

And at some point – and I cannot fathom how – he learned the wordcraft that won him the praise of wealthier travellers.

And one day, he must have decided that he wanted something more than a dirty life in the ditches and stale ponds of the kingdom, so decided to come to the King's Castle. As you can imagine, when Throch first plodded up to the south gate to the town that surrounded the castle, the people walking along the road to and from the town were quite disgusted by him. Slime from the ponds he had slept in still clung to the now copper-green ermine cloak that he wore. Greasy sweat from his mushroomed feet stained the hard earth of the road dark brown.

Although it should be said that one thing they weren't disgusted by so much was the smell. All trolls stink, of course. No two trolls smell alike, but they all smell of some mixture of rotten chicken, blue cheese, oil paint that has been mixed with water and left to stand for a month, apricot (curiously, though it does little to stay the other aromas), vomit, and shit. All trolls, that is, except for Throch. You see, Throch liked fragrances – all kinds. Many of the lords and ladies who met him upon the road, sitting in their ornate carriages, said later that the one thing Throch asked them for most was perfume.

What Throch did not have, however, was a good taste in fragrances. He would drench himself with every fragrance he owned at once. This resulted in an overpowering concoction that left most gasping for the stale air of a sewer. However, it was redeemed in that it was better than what trolls usually smell of.

The King's Castle and the town around it are surrounded by a great wall. It is fifteen feet high and seven feet thick. There are only three ways through it: the north gate, the west gate, and the south gate. On this day, when this story starts, there were three cats sitting atop the wall, bathing in the summer sunlight. One was ginger and white, one was black and white, and one was tabby. It should be noted that trolls do not fear cats, as many other foul beings do, but it is thought that this is simply because they are too stupid. Cats certainly detest trolls, and upon smelling the thick air that wafted from the direction of Throch, these three cats got up, and walked off – no doubt to go and sleep on a feather bed somewhere in the castle.

Each of the three gates in the great wall that surrounds the town was guarded by fifteen of the King's Loyal Guards. When they saw the eight-foot-tall troll stomping up to the gate, they rushed to fight it off. They would have killed him within a minute (for they were most skilled) or at least fought him back to the woods a way from the town, but Throch was cunning.

When the first Loyal Guard strode up to Throch (who was investigating a piece of trout that had become lodged between the largest and second-largest toes of his right foot eight days ago), he said 'Oi! Leave here you filthy troll, or I'll slice open your eight stomachs!' He shouted this at Throch, because most trolls are both dim-witted and partly deaf.

Throch, however, had excellent hearing. He turned his head sharply, and a few pieces of brown-yellow straw fell off. 'That is a most rude thing to say', he gargled. 'I am just walking along this road, minding my own business.'

'Be it rude or not', said the Loyal Guard, whose name was Cyneweard, 'you may not come to this town.' And he raised his sword and pointed it at Throch, to restate his earlier threat.

'And now you are threatening me with a sword', Throch said, quite calmly. 'And yet I have done nothing unlawful.'

'Your presence here is unlawful', Cyneweard responded.

'Where is your evidence of that?' Throch interjected, masterfully irate. 'Can you show me this law? Do you have it written on a piece of vellum in your hand? Unless you can prove at this moment that this is the law, then you have no right to threaten me with stomach-cutting, and I have every right to simply walk along this road harming no-one.'

'It is common knowledge that trolls may not enter towns.' the Loyal Guard said hastily.

'And do you think "common knowledge" is the same as law?' Throch said as he towered over the guard.

'No-'

'Well then clearly you are being absurd.' Throch said. 'Why are you putting so much effort into harassing innocent businessmen such as myself? Why aren't you doing anything to stop the Northumbrians who wander so freely through your gates?!'

Now this was clever of Throch. Most people hated the Northumbrians. They hated trolls more, but the Northumbrian invasion three years before had left a resentment for those northern folk, some of whom came to the King's Castle to trade.

'The Northumbrians are welcome here-' Cyneweard began again.

'And yet they have attacked many of the towns along the border of the kingdom over the last few months! They have invaded before and they will attempt to invade again! They would see this kingdom brought to ruin! The Northumbrians are savage, foul, and uncivilised, and yet they are allowed into this town but my right to walk here is threatened!'

By this time, many of the people who had been walking along the road, passing through the great stone wall, had stopped to watch and listen to the troll.

Cyneweard stumbled, and before he could respond to Throch, a second guard, whose name was Eadweard (and who was, incidentally, the fifth son of the fourth son of the brother of King Eadric, and so a distant cousin of King Aethelraed), stepped forward. He said 'If we allow Northumbrians into our town then I see no reason why we should not let this troll into our town, as long as he does not thieve or attack anyone.'

'But he is a troll!' Cyneweard said. 'Of course he will do as such!' to which many of the townsfolk standing around the two guards and the one troll murmured in agreement.

'And yet the Northumbrians have attacked us far more than trolls have over the last few years, and we allow them into the town.'

Even more townsfolk grumbled in agreement to that.

'Northumbrians should be banned from entering the kingdom.' Throch said. 'And any that come here should be cut in three!'

A few townsfolk cheered in agreement, but more said nothing.

'You may go about the town, troll', Eadweard said, 'so long as you obey the king's laws.'

'Of course, of course', Throch grunted.

'Then go onwards', Eadweard said, standing aside to let the troll through the gate.

And so Throch walked into the town.

Throch walked along the busy main street, and after a way he came to a tavern. While he had lived in the countryside, by roads and under bridges, most of Throch's meals had been raw fish, frogspawn stew, roasted toads, and occasionally cold salted ham or mouldy bread. With the chance to eat fresher food, Throch shuffled into the tavern.

When Throch pushed the heavy oak door to the tavern open with one hand, those already inside jumped off their seats – unaware that this particular troll had been permitted to enter the town.

A blacksmith, who sat at a table in the corner of the tavern, said 'Oi! Leave here you filthy troll, or I shall call upon the King's Loyal Guards to come and drain the grey blood from your veins!'

'That is a most rude thing to say.' he glugged. 'I have just come in here for a drink and some bread – I am just minding my own business.'

'Be it rude or not', the blacksmith said, 'you may not come into this tavern. We want no trolls here. You will most likely try to steal food and drink.'

'And now you are accusing me of a crime I have not committed.' Throch said, quite calmly. 'And yet I have done nothing unlawful.'

'Your presence here is unlawful.' the blacksmith said.

'On the contrary', Throch began, 'I have been given permission to go about the town freely by the king's guards.'

'That is true.' said a young farmer, who had been in the crowd around the troll earlier. 'I can attest that this troll has been permitted to wander the town freely by the king's own men.'

'You see.' Throch said. 'I am an honest person, and yet this man', he said, pointing at the blacksmith with a gnarled, greasy finger and speaking to the whole room, 'has accused me of crimes I did not commit.'

'I did not accuse you of committing a cr-'

'Then you are saying that I have committed no crimes?' Throch interjected.

'Yes but-'

'But what?' Throch interjected. 'You are accusing me of being a dishonest person and yet I see that it is *you* who is dishonest. You must be a goldsmith. Only goldsmiths are so dishonest.'

'I am a blacksmith.' the blacksmith said hastily.

'Have you thought about a change of craft?' Throch said. Many around the tavern laughed. 'Your dishonesty would make you the perfect goldsmith! You could cheat people out of their gold by swapping it for fool's gold.'

Many more around the room guffawed. The blacksmith tried to respond, but he could not be heard over the raucous laughter.

Throch ignored the blacksmith, and sat down at a squat table, his flabby arse swallowing the seat beneath him. The tavernkeeper brought him a drink, placing it on the oak table at an arm's length to avoid breathing in the troll's sickly stench. A wealthy merchant from Essex came over to the troll.

'You are right about goldsmiths.' the merchant said. 'They do so often cheat others out of their money.'

'If the king had any sense', Throch began, 'he would have them all hanged for their dishonesty and thievery.'

'Indeed', the wealthy merchant said. 'You are most wise. Allow me to buy you your drink, and this tavern's finest pork pie.'

'You are most generous.' Throch said. 'This kingdom needs more fine folk like you.'

The tavernkeeper brought the troll a pork pie, and bread, and some sweet fruit cakes, and much more food that the wealthy merchant paid for.

Once Throch had finished eating, he lolloped out of the tavern, and continued along the street.

After a way he came to the market square. Hundreds of carts stood on the golden stone of the square as common folk from the lands around the castle had come to sell wheat, barley, leather, and wool. They leapt back at the sound of the troll – his squelching arse and his clapping thighs – but they had already learned from the king's guards that the troll had been permitted to wander the town.

Throch went from cart to cart, inspecting the items that each seller sold. He would pick the items up with his oily hands, turn them over several times, sniff them, and then drop them back onto the cart. Throch was never known to have had or spent any money, so most likely he had no intention of actually buying any of these items. Nevertheless he went from cart to cart and befilthed the bread and vegetables, coats and armour on each.

Knowing how strong the troll probably was, most of the sellers said nothing, and just hoped the troll would move on as quickly as possible. Once he had passed, they quickly rinsed off the black mould he had smeared onto their goods.

One seller – a grey-haired woman selling linens – would not stand for the troll doing this, however. When she saw the troll gradually moving along to her cart (as he was currently inspecting some pottery) she said 'Oi! Get your filthy hands off these goods you fetid troll! Go away! Leave this market and leave this town! Go back to the shitty puddle you came from!'

'That is a most rude thing to say.' the troll slurped. 'I have just come to this market to see the fine pottery and jewellery produced by the most excellent people of this town, but now you are demanding that I leave the town just because you are offended by my presence. Needless to say, there are many people who are offended by your presence too – no-one wants to have to look at a grey, wrinkled, old woman, who is probably twice-widowed, like you.'

The market square was busy, and though none stood within three long paces of the troll, many townsfolk pressed against each other as they stood and watched the troll and the old woman.

'My husband is alive and well, and he is well thought of by all.' the old woman said.

'Your husband may be alive, but I doubt he is well with a bitch like you for a wife.' Throch said. Several around the troll laughed out of surprise. 'I imagine he has suffered through a long depression, being married to you. Why, if I had the misfortune of you as a wife, I would have killed myself years ago!'

'That's rich, coming from you.' the old woman said. 'I imagine most people vomit at the thought of marrying you – just for your smell, let alone your odorous words.'

Many in the audience around them agreed, of course, though none said so.

'A typical woman.' Throch said. 'You are offended by my honest words, and yet I recall that it was you who tried to insult me first. Such hypocrisy. You are a typical old woman – bitter, self-centred, and controlling.'

Two or three of those standing around the troll agreed loudly. The rest were silent.

'And you are a typical troll.' the old woman retorted. 'You are arrogant, fat, foul-'

'You see!' Throch interjected. 'Once again, you are apparently allowed to say whatever you like to me, yet I am apparently not allowed to speak truthfully to you. Such hypocrisy. Only women are known to be such hypocrites.'

A wealthy lord, who happened to have been passing through the market square with several of his own guards, and who had been standing among the crowd around the troll, stepped forwards before the old woman could respond.

'Let us not forget the King's Law.' the wealthy lord said. 'You may not like what someone says, but they are completely free to say it.' he said to the old woman. 'This troll has been given permission to go about the town – under the King's Law, he may not be driven from it just because of something he has said.'

Unwilling to try to argue against a wealthy and powerful lord, the old woman said nothing, and the crowd around them began to disperse.

The wealthy lord turned to the troll and said quietly 'You are right about women. They take offence so easily, and they should not be allowed to participate in discussions of the matters of greater importance, for they cannot reason as well as men.'

'If the king were not so easily swayed by the words of his queen', Throch said, 'he would order all women to remain silent unless asked to speak by a man, else her tongue be cut out and fed to pigs.'

'Indeed', the wealthy lord said. 'You are most wise. Allow me to take you to my house; for as long as you stay in the town, you may stay there.'

And so the wealthy lord brought Throch to his house, which was a very large house close to the outer wall of the

King's Castle. The wealthy lord had many spare rooms, and plenty more food. Throch took the room that he liked the most, and the lord's servants brought the troll more to eat throughout the evening.

The next day, when the troll awoke, the wealthy lord invited him to come to the King's Castle. King Aethelraed held a great council every week, at which any man or woman, be they noble or common, was welcome to attend and to speak. The king would listen to the plights of all, and use what he heard to make decisions for the good of the kingdom – a wise course of action, until it came to Throch.

The wealthy lord and his guards walked through the gates of the King's Castle to the great hall that King Aethelraed had constructed for these councils. Throch tried to follow them.

'Halt!' said one of the King's Loyal Guards who stood by the gate. 'You may have been permitted to go about the town, troll, but you may not enter this great hall.'

'And why is that?' Throch oozed.

'This is where folk both common and noble discuss ideas for the betterment of the whole kingdom. Doubtless the only ideas you will have are of theft and murder.'

'And have you *heard* any of my ideas?' the troll said.

'I have not.' the guard responded. 'But you are a troll, and trolls only think about such things.'

'So you are trying to silence me and yet you have not heard any of my ideas?' Throch said. 'I have only been in this town for a day, and yet I have already met many people who agree with me. It seems you are just trying to silence a point of view that you don't like. Need I remind you that it is the King's Law that anyone may say whatever they like without persecution – are you trying to break the King's Law?'

'Of course not.'

'Then you must allow people with different points of view to you to speak, and you must permit them to enter this great hall.'

The Loyal Guard could not disagree with the troll. The troll had been permitted to go about the town, as long as he did not thieve or attack, and indeed the troll had not done so. While many had complained about what the troll had said thus far, the troll was within his rights within the King's Law.

'Very well', the Loyal Guard said, 'you may enter the great hall, and be part of the debate.'

And so Throch stomped into the great hall.

The great hall that Aethelraed had built for these great councils was (and still is) magnificent. The room within it is by far the longest in the kingdom, at a hundred yards. During these great councils, most of the common and noble folk sit or stand on the ground floor, which is paved with marble, but there is more space on a first floor balcony where yet more common and noble folk stand side by side. At the far end is a dais, where the king and his ministers sit and listen to all.

Thousands of people were already inside the great hall when Throch came in. Upon smelling Throch's thick, floral scent, those standing around him pushed up against the walls of the hall so as to stand at least five long paces away from the foul troll. (Those who came in after the troll were careful to step over the moist, shitty stains the troll left on the floor.)

King Aethelraed, who was already seated on the throne upon the dais, had sharp eyesight, and saw the troll from the far end of the room. His Loyal Guards had already told him of the troll's presence within the town, and the king had agreed that so long as the troll did not break any laws, the troll could go about the town as he liked. Indeed, King Aethelraed wondered that if trolls didn't break any laws at all, was there really any problem with them?

The King's Herald called the great council to order, and all in the hall were silent.

King Aethelraed stood. His great red cloak swayed and the gold crown upon his head glinted in the sunlight that pierced the high windows of the hall.

'I welcome you all to this great council.' the king said. 'A king must have advisers, and surely the more advisers a king has, the better his decisions can be. Good ideas can come from anyone. Thus you are all my advisers, and I welcome all of your ideas. Speak now of your plights, and what must be done to resolve them.'

'Your majesty', a carpenter said, 'I come from a small town twelve leagues to the west of here. In recent months we have seen many Britons from the west come to our lands. The harvests of recent years have not provided them with the food they need. These people need food, water, and somewhere to sleep, but we cannot provide this to them ourselves. Would your majesty send extra provisions to the west of the kingdom so that these newcomers may not starve?'

The king was about to respond – he looked as though he was going to agree with the carpenter, and his scribe was already writing down the request. But before King Aethelraed could respond, Throch spoke.

'I don't see why we should help these people.' he spat. 'The Britons would not do the same for us if we had need of their help. They are not our problem, and we should not give our precious food to them. Many in this kingdom too have suffered through the past few years – we do not have the food to give.'

Many around the troll agreed.

'That is untrue.' the carpenter said. 'We have had many good harvests over the last few years. The soil of our land is rich. We have the food to sp-'

'You do not deny the fact that the Britons would not give us food if we went to them and asked for it. The Britons are savage, foul, and uncivilised. If we give them this food and water, they would see this kingdom as weak, and would immediately invade.'

The same people around the troll agreed with him again.

'It does not matter if-' the carpenter began.

'It does not matter if they invade?' the troll exclaimed. 'I think there are many people who have had to fight off invaders over the years who would disagree with you.'

The same people around the troll agreed with him a third time.

'No, it does not matter if they would do the s-' the carpenter began again.

'Any Briton that crosses the border into this kingdom should be cut in three!' the troll shouted.

Many around the troll were shocked by the troll's remark, and called for the troll to leave.

'Your majesty', the carpenter began again, turning to the king, 'this is ridiculous. Why has this troll been allowed into this great hall?'

'What's ridiculous is that apparently you can't listen to the opinions of people who disagree with you!' Throch said loudly. 'Apparently anyone's allowed to speak in this hall as long as they speak the right words!'

'That is not what I said.'

'That's exactly what you said! You're offended and you don't like being offended so you don't want the people around you to say the things that offend you. This is hardly in concurrence with the King's Law.'

'Your majesty I must agree with the troll.' one of the king's guards said, before the carpenter could respond. The guard's name was Eadweard – the same guard that Throch had met when he first arrived at the gates of the town. 'He has done nothing unlawful, and he must be permitted to speak freely, as we all are. He should not be thrown from this great hall simply because we disagree with him.'

'I agree that this troll has the right to speak freely, under my own laws', the king said to his distant cousin, 'but this opinion is very different to what most people in this hall seem to think on the matter. Why should we spend time discussing ideas that most here would not ever imagine doing?'

'Your majesty that is exactly why we *should* listen to what this troll has to say. If we are all speaking the same words, where do the new ideas come from? Furthermore, while some in this hall do not agree with the troll, there are clearly also many who do.'

'Very well', the king said, 'the troll may remain.'

'Your majesty', the carpenter began, 'you cannot seriously be considering doing what the troll says? Though we have fought the Britons many times over the last centuries, the people coming to ours lands now are not our enemies.'

'I have no intention of killing these Britons, for you are right – they are not our enemies. I will send as much wheat and barley as is necessary to the west to provide for them. However, all have the right to speak freely in this hall, and throughout my kingdom. I too disagree with the troll, but to throw him from this hall would go against my own decree. Therefore, he must be allowed to stay and speak as he wishes, and we must all listen.'

Everyone in the hall agreed with the king.

Throch said little throughout the remainder of the great council – those who were there and who recount this story say that he seemed uninterested in the other matters brought to the king's attention.

For the next week Throch stayed at the house of the wealthy lord he had met in the market square. The troll was costly to keep – servants brought him food constantly for twelve hours of the day. At first this was fine fruits and cakes, but after a few days the lord's servants realised that they could provide the troll with less food if they gave him foods that were somewhat more difficult to eat, so they gave him fatty meats seasoned with mustard and rosemary. Trolls certainly do not become less disgusting when they are given beds to sleep on and baths to wash in. Many have told of how, for the time that the troll stayed at the lord's house, the air in the street beside it smelled strongly floral and fungal.

Some days Throch would spend his time doing nothing other than eating, shitting, and sleeping, not leaving the lord's house at all. Other days he would wander the town, causing just as much disruption as he had on the first day he was there, though he never did any of the things that trolls are known to do often, such as threaten people into giving them things. He needed no more food, of course (not that trolls are ever known to be contented), but he did not steal any jewellery or perfume, nor did he attack anyone.

King Aethelraed saw this as a good sign. Perhaps some trolls were simply not as troublesome as most were.

Though he did notice the gifts that the wealthy lord and others were giving to the troll.

A week later, and King Aethelraed presided over the next great council. This time, Throch had no difficulty getting into the great hall. No-one stopped him, and no-one questioned it. Throch also went to the great hall earlier in the day, and so stood much closer to the king's dais than he had done the week before.

The King's Herald called the great council to order, and all in the hall were silent.

King Aethelraed stood. His great red cloak swayed and the gold crown upon his head glinted in the sunlight that pierced the high windows of the hall.

'I welcome you all to this great council.' the king said. 'A king must have advisers, and surely the more advisers a king has, the better his decisions can be. Good ideas can come from anyone. Thus you are all my advisers, and I welcome all of your ideas. Speak now of your plights, and what must be done to resolve them.'

Many matters were brought to the king's attention: an increase in theft in Hwitwaeter, a supposed dragon in the east that needed to be slain, and the need to rebuild several bridges across the Afon and the Cirne. On all of these matters, Throch remained silent. After many had spoken, one of the king's own scholars spoke.

'Your majesty', the scholar said, 'there is another matter that I would like to bring to your attention. Over the last eight years we have observed a decrease in the amount of rainfall over late summer. It may be a good idea to build a series of reservoirs upstream on the Trent, to hold back some of the water from earlier in the year so that it may be used for irrigation later in the year.'

No-one in the great hall raised an objection to this, and once again the King's Scribe was about to write down the idea for the king to review later, when Throch spoke.

'What an outrageous proposal!' Throch began. 'You would spend our money building reservoirs just to hold back the water we have a right to?! People need that water, and who are you to say when and how they might use it?! You should stay out of such things. It is for each man to decide for himself. Besides, I think we can all agree that there has been no shortage of water over the last few years. Why, over the last few months alone, it has rained almost every day!'

A few people in the hall – mainly the lords and ladies – agreed with the troll.

'That's not what I said.' the scholar replied. 'I said that there was less rain over *late summer* – not late spring and early summer. We've had plenty of rain over the last few months, but over the next few months, based on what we've seen over th-'

'Everyone can see that there has been plenty of rain – too much rain. There is no shortage of water, but if you tax people to build reservoirs, there will be a shortage of coin!' Throch retorted.

The same people in the hall agreed with the troll again.

'You are an idiot if you think that's what I'm say-'

'Oh *I'm* an idiot am I? We're all idiots are we just because we look to the skies and see rain? This is the typical arrogance of these so-called "scholars". They think that *they* are so intelligent and that *we* are so stupid. They pretend that they are so knowledgeable because they are so *educated*, but they know nothing more than the common man, and sometimes less. If these people are going to keep making false statements, their money should be taken from them and they should be thrown from the town.'

Many around the troll were shocked by the troll's remark, and called for the troll to leave.

'Your majesty', the scholar began, 'this is ridiculous. I know that the troll has the right to say what he likes, but every opinion he has is of attacking others. We have no need of such opinions.'

'What's ridiculous is that apparently you can't listen to the opinions of people who disagree with you!' Throch said loudly. 'Apparently anyone's allowed to speak in this hall as long as they speak the right words!'

'That is not what I said.'

'That's exactly what you said! You're offended and you don't like being offended so you don't want the people around you to say the things that offend you. This is hardly in concurrence with the King's Law.'

'Your majesty I must agree with the troll', a wealthy merchant said – the same wealthy merchant who Throch had met in the tavern the week before. 'He must be allowed to speak freely. Indeed, we must listen to what the troll has to say.'

'I agree that this troll has the right to speak freely, under my own laws', the king said, 'but the decisions that I take must be just, and I will do no harm to those who have not earned it. Given that the troll's opinions differ from mine and most of those in this hall, why should we spend time discussing ideas that most here would not ever imagine doing?'

'Your majesty that is exactly why we *should* listen to the troll. We cannot gain wisdom by listening to those we already agree with. We can only gain wisdom by listening to those we disagree with. Given that there are clearly many people in this hall who agree with the troll, I recommend that the troll be made a minister, so as to provide a balance of opinions among your ministers.'

Many in the hall were shocked at this suggestion; they murmured among themselves and shouted disapproval at the merchant. And they were right to be shocked. Until a week ago, no troll had ever set foot in the King's Castle, yet now one might become a minister for the king.

'There is already balance among the opinions of my ministers.' the king said.

'Clearly there is not, your majesty.' the merchant said. 'Else the troll's opinions would not seem so unusual.'

King Aethelraed thought on that for a moment, and then said 'Very well. Since there are many here who agree with the troll on this and other matters, the troll shall be a minister.'

There was yet more outrage in the hall as the king called for another chair to be brought onto the dais. The king raised a hand to call for silence in the hall as Throch, without saying anything, plodded forward to the dais, and sat on the chair.

The remainder of the great council was uneasy. Unlike the week before, Throch commented on almost every matter that was brought forth. Most of the time, he was in favour of doing nothing. When solving the problem involved spending tax money, Throch was utterly outraged. He disagreed with the king's ministers on almost everything, and for every matter, there was no resolution – the King's Scribe could write down nothing other than to come to the matter again at the next great council. When normally King Aethelraed might have decided upon a course of action that would swiftly resolve each problem, he was now persuaded to delay action, or take no action at all.

The great council was called to an end once again. Those who left the great hall were malcontent – the very sort of malcontent that these great councils were intended to abate.

Over the next week, Throch's life was very different, once again, to what it had been the week before. Throch continued to live in the house of the wealthy lord he had met eight days before, but now he was plied with even more rich food than he had been in the first week: honey-glazed pork, ribeye beef steak, blackberry jam tarts, and clotted cream on bread. The wealthy lord spared no expense on the troll, even buying him eight bottles of perfume every day and chains of gold inlaid with rubies, for now the troll was a minister, and the lord had a voice in the royal court (where before he had not).

Not only this, but many others seemed to forget the troll's flowery stench. Many visited the troll during the week, among them the wealthy merchant and Eadweard the guard who had spoken for Throch in the last two great councils. The troll was also often visited by those among the townsfolk who agreed with the troll's outrageous opinions – only a small fraction of the total number of people in the town, but large enough to fill the street outside the wealthy lord's house. Every evening Throch would stand outside the door to the house, on the stone steps, and speak to his followers, who grew more and more numerous each day. Throch said many of the same things to them that he said in the great councils. He called for any Northumbrians in the kingdom to be cut in three, and when the crowd cheered at that, he called for the king to march into Northumbria and take the lands for Mercia. He called for any woman who tried to speak over anyone else to have her tongue cut out, and when the crowd cheered that, he called for women to be banned from speaking entirely.

Also unlike the previous week, Throch did not spend so much of the day at the house of the wealthy lord. Now that Throch was a minister, each day he went into the King's Castle, and sat with the other lords of the royal court at the great round table that Aethelraed had built in the first year of his reign. There the king and his ministers would discuss the details of the affairs of state.

Throch was far less fiery at these gatherings of the royal court than he was when he spoke to his followers in the evenings. He was sullen, and uninterested. Most of what was said he did not comment on. When he did comment, it was only to dismiss ideas with little conviction. Indeed, many of the other ministers at those gatherings have told of how the troll did not seem particularly intelligent, and could not grasp the complexities of the subjects.

After another week had passed, King Aethelraed held another great council. Hundreds of common folk shuffled into the great hall – many from around the town, but many who had come from towns far away in order to speak before the king. Throch lolloped into the great hall too – this time only once everyone else had arrived – he pushed his way through the crowd to the dais, and sat upon his stained chair to the right of the king.

The King's Herald called the great council to order, and all in the hall were silent.

King Aethelraed stood. His great red cloak swayed and the gold crown upon his head glinted in the sunlight that pierced the high windows of the hall.

'I welcome you all to this great council.' the king said. 'A king must have advisers, and surely the more advisers a king has, the-'

'Oh we don't need to do all that again.' Throch said loudly. Many gasped in shock.

Had anyone interrupted the king during King Eadric's or King Eadthryth's day, they would have had their tongue cut out. King Aethelraed, ever patient and calm, however, did not mind. 'Very well', he said. 'Let us begin.'

Many matters were brought to the king's attention, but it took a long time to get through each one. Throch contested every point. He questioned the motivations of each speaker. He claimed that each person who spoke was motivated only by greed and spite – they sought only to enrich themselves at the expense of others. Whenever someone asked for extra food or water, or for bridges to be built or rebuilt, or for roads to be maintained, he argued that the king should not interfere with such matters – that it was for the people to do these things themselves. Throch many times called for the king to invade Northumbria or Essex or Sussex.

Throch was adored by some and despised by others. With each remark he made, many of those in the great hall booed the troll, while his followers cheered loudly. In these times, the great councils of King Aethelraed were very different to how they were previously: serene and direct.

Nothing was decided upon. The king's ministers (not including Throch) grew more and more frustrated with each matter that was brought before the king. It took so long to debate each matter, that the king cut the debate short each time, so as to make progress.

After many hours of debate, a young boy stepped forward to speak to the king. The boy was fourteen years old. He had long, brown, wavy hair that was tied back with a red band. His skin was white and smooth, and his linen clothes had been embroidered with dragons and flowers, lions and swans.

'Your majesty', the boy said, 'I come from the town of Tiwesburg. There has been much theft in the town over the last few months, but we are unable to seize or fight off the thieves. Would your majesty send some able fighters to the town to apprehend the thieves?'

Before King Aethelraed was able to respond, Throch spoke. 'What is going on here?' he said, looking at the boy with a smirk of curiosity. The crowd could sense what was about to happen. Throch laughed at the boy. 'Are you a boy or a girl?'

The crowd waited nervously. 'A boy.' the boy said.

Throch snorted. 'You certainly don't look like one.'

Some among the crowd laughed hard at the troll's remark. The rest remained silent.

'Why are you wearing girl's clothes?' the troll asked.

'I'm not.' the boy said.

'Oh please', the troll replied, 'what kind of boy wears clothes with so much embroidery on them? And is your hair braided?'

The same people among the crowd laughed hard again.

'What in all the land does that have to do with the boy's question?' one of the king's other ministers asked.

'Quite a lot it would seem', the troll said. 'If this boy or girl or whatever it is cannot defend itself from a few thieves, then clearly it cannot be a boy, as it claims to be.'

'That still has nothing to do with the boy's question, which was whether the king can send some men at arms to Tiwesburg to apprehend these thieves.' the king's other minister retorted.

'Clearly the boys and men of Tiwesburg are not truly boys and men at all.' Throch said, to cheers and shouts and jeers and boos from those within the hall. 'They are weak! Why should they depend on their king to deal with such matters?! If they can't deal with thieves on their own then they are weak, and deserve everything they get!'

'It is the king's duty to defend his p-'

'This is clearly the result of Saxon influence! This is what happens when you let Saxons take your land! All of the men and boys start thinking they are women and girls!'

By this point Throch himself was shouting over the clamour of the crowd in the great hall.

'The Saxons would have us destroy our kingdom from within!' Throch shouted. 'They must be driven from the land – that is the only way to preserve the civility of the Angles and the Britons!'

The king, who had been listening intently, turned towards Throch. 'Britons?' he said.

'Yes', the troll replied. 'When it was just the Britons and the Angles in this part of Albion, it was a far more civilised place.'

'But you said the Britons were savage, foul, and uncivilised.' the king said. King Aethelraed had an excellent memory, and could remember just about everything anyone said.

The crowd became quieter again.

'So?' said the troll.

'So how can you think both of these things at the same time? They are contradictory.'

'That doesn't matter.' the troll said loudly. 'Consistency is not important.'

And in that moment, King Aethelraed the Wise realised what the troll was doing. In that moment, he was finally able to see through the troll's cunning.

Throch didn't say the things that he said because he *believed* them – he said them because they got a reaction. Throch had no interest in trying to resolve any of the matters brought before the king. He simply said outrageous things in order to keep the attention on himself. For as long as the attention was on Throch, the troll would keep being given fine food, clothing, jewellery, and perfume. *That* was what the troll wanted.

King Aethelraed turned to his Loyal Guards. 'Seize him.'

The King's Loyal Guards rushed towards the troll, spears in hand. Within a moment he was surrounded.

'How DARE you!' Throch shouted at the king, for the first time irate but not in control.

'Remove him from this hall.' the king said.

'That is utter hypocrisy!' the troll shouted. He turned to the crowd. 'This is persecution! By the king's own decree I may say what I like without persecution!' He turned back to the king. 'You are just trying to silence an opinion you don't like!'

'By your own admission, you will say one thing one moment and its opposite the next. Perhaps the things you say are indeed your opinions; perhaps they are not – we have no way of knowing if anything you have ever said is truly your opinion. How can I possibly be trying to silence a point of view when we don't even know what that point of view is? You have no interest in solving the problems that are brought before me in this hall. That is the entire point of these great councils: to make decisions for the betterment of the kingdom. It is entirely a waste of time to have anyone in such a council who does not believe that the suggestions they are making are correct. You say the things you say to provoke outrage. Outrage brings you attention; attention brings you gifts. You are manipulating the debate for attention – that is your entire purpose here.' the king said.

'I HAVE A RIGHT TO SAY WHAT I LIKE!!!' Throch screamed.

'Yes, you do.' the king replied. 'But you do not have a right to any audience of your choosing.'

And so the king's skilful men at arms forced the troll from the hall with spear and sword. Throch continued screaming about his right to speak and his alleged persecution as he was driven backwards. Everyone else in the hall was silent as the troll was removed, including his former supporters, Eadweard, the wealthy merchant, and the wealthy lord.

Though Throch was eight feet tall and five times as heavy as the king's heaviest guardsman, Throch was not ferocious in his fight back against the king's men at arms. He swiped at them a few times, but when he cut his arms on their spears, his vanity (for Throch thought himself truly beautiful, and did not want to scar his skin) prevented him from holding his ground.

Throch was driven from the great hall, and then from the King's Castle, and then from the town that surrounded the castle, back out through the same gate he had entered through. King Aethelraed followed his skilled men at arms, a few paces away, as this happened, and his people followed behind him. Once the king's men at arms had fought the troll back through the gate, onto the road south of the town, they stopped, and formed a wall of themselves.

'I HAVE A RIGHT TO ENTER THE TOWN!!!' Throch screamed.

'No, you don't.' the king said. 'You have a right to say what you like and not be persecuted for it. And you may do that here. On the roads of my kingdom you may say whatever you like, and no-one may strike or kill you for it. But you may not come to this town, nor any other town in my kingdom.'

Throch continued shouting at the king, and even called for him to be overthrown. But the king turned, and walked back to the castle, with his people behind him. The King's Loyal Guards stayed at the gate, spears in hand, to ensure that the troll did not come back into the town.

Throch stayed outside of the town for many days. At first, his supporters, who had previously come to hear the troll speak outside the lord's house, came to listen to the troll outside the walls of the town. But with each passing day, fewer and fewer came, as each began to notice more and more contradictions in the things Throch said, and as each saw that all Throch truly wanted was fine clothes, jewellery, and perfume.

Many came to the town from lands far away who had not heard the troll speak before, and some were enamoured with the troll's words. When they asked why the troll was not allowed into the town, however, the townsfolk explained all that had happened, and the newcomers too began to see through the troll's words, and see what he truly wanted.

As fewer and fewer people came to listen to the troll, Throch became bored, and wandered away again. And after this, not much more is known of Throch. He went back to harassing lords and ladies along the roads, and while there were some who still supported him, as he had been banished from the towns of the kingdom, he was of little use to them. Aside from this, Throch was never seen or heard of again, and it is assumed that at some point he died in a ditch.

The reign of King Aethelraed the Great after that was, for the most part, a peaceful and prosperous one. Throch had caused many problems for the king – in the weeks when the troll was part of the king's great councils, and when he was one of the king's ministers, many actions that would have been taken weren't. But the king, in his wisdom, was eventually able to see the troll's true intentions. If only the king had not trusted the troll to begin with, it would all have been avoided.

King Aethelraed learned that both fame and infamy had their rewards, and that sometimes, those rewards were all that someone wanted, regardless of how they got them. He learned that by allowing the troll to speak so often in the great hall – far more than any other one person – and by making the troll a minister, he had given the troll more attention – and that was what the troll had wanted. Throch had manipulated the king into giving him more attention.

And ultimately, King Aethelraed learned the most important thing about trolls: don't trust them. Don't listen to them; don't talk to them; don't give them any attention. To put it simply:

Don't. Feed. The trolls.

# The Troll With No Name

This story happened some time during the reign of King Hereweald. No-one seems to know what year it was – there have been countless retellings of this tale – each one slightly different.

Trolls can often be found in ditches and ponds – and under bridges, of course. Some trolls have been known to dwell in small huts in dark forests made out of stone or wood covered in mud and pig shit. One might call those the more civilised trolls. But during the reign of King Hereweald, there was one troll who chose to live in a stone hut by the side of the King's Road.

He had built the stone hut himself. No-one had seen him do it, but the walls were thick – eight feet thick by some reckonings. The hut had no door, thus no-one could get inside to kill the troll, but seemingly he also could not get out. The area around the hut reportedly stank overpoweringly of shit, so it seems that this was true.

The troll did not need to get out, however. Sometimes people travelling along the King's Road would appease the troll by throwing a leg of mutton or hard black bread over the tall walls of the hut, so the troll always had food. Later, once the troll was gone, it was found that he had built the hut around a well, and so always had water too.

Thus there was no way in or out of the hut. In fact, there was only one gap in the walls of the hut – too narrow for a spear or a sword, but wide enough to shout through.

Many people travel along the King's Road. Reeves and thanes from the west of the kingdom often travel along it to the King's Castle. Merchants often travel along the road, going from town to town, selling cloths and jewellery and fragrances. And many common folk walk along the road too.

One of the people to come across the troll in the hut was a woman named Mildthryth – the wife of a farmer. She was carrying many heavy bags of wheat on a cart to the nearby town of Thoresburg to sell them.

Mildthryth and her husband did not have much money, and could not afford to buy an ox to pull the cart for them. They owned no gold or silver jewellery, and their woollen clothes were old, torn, and muddy. Mildthryth was in her forties. Her skin was brown from the sun and the dirt in which she, her husband, and her two daughters toiled all day in the summer months.

'EEEUUUGGGHHH!!!' shouted the troll in the hut when Mildthryth walked past it, dragging the heavy cart down the road. The earth of the road had baked under the summer sun, and the mud had dried to make shallow valleys and mountains, which trapped the wheels of the cart.

'Who said that?' Mildthryth shouted towards the hut. 'Who's there?'

'You're disGUSting!' the troll shouted again, through the narrow gap in the walls of his hut. 'Maybe try eating less food, you fat fucking pig. And get some better clothes – no-one'll want to fuck you if you're wearing that!'

'I am not want for your foul words!' Mildthryth said. 'Where are you?'

'I'm over 'ere!'

'What, in the hut?'

'No, I'm sitting on a winged fucking horse – of course I'm in my castle! Are you stupid as well as ugly?'

'You must be a troll!' Mildthryth said.

'I'll take that as a yes.' the troll glugged.

'Leave this roadside! You are not welcome here!'

'I shall not leave this roadside. This is where I live. Now go and put some better clothes on, so that I might look out of my castle on a nicer sight than you. And bring me bread and ham and honey.'

'I will bring you no food, you arrogant, unpleasant troll!'

'Then give me gold. Clearly you 'ave gold to spare, as you 'aven't spent it on clothes or jewellery.'

'I have no gold, and even if I did I would not give it to you! You are a disgusting, filthy troll!'

'I may be filthy, but you are old and wrinkled! If you have daughters, go and bring me them so that I may look at something that is more worthy of my attention!'

'Do not speak of my daughters again, you fetid, arrogant troll! I shall tell the King's Guards of you when they next pass this way! They will be rid of you! What is your name?'

'My name is the Dragon-Slayer of Wessex.' the troll said proudly.

'That is no troll-name!' Mildthryth replied. 'What is your real name?'

'That is indeed my real name. That is how I am known throughout the kingdom. Mention my name to any swordsman or great warrior in the land, and he shall know that "The Dragon-Slayer of Wessex" means me.'

'I am not a fool.' Mildthryth said. 'I know that is not your real name. But it matters not. I will tell the King's Guards that you are here anyway, and they will come, and they will smash down the walls of your hut and kill you.'

'You *are* a fool. No man can break down the walls of my castle, for I have built them thick and tall and strong.'

'We shall see.' Mildthryth said, and she continued pulling her cart along the uneven road, while the troll hurled more insults at her, until she was out of sight.

Fortunately, when Mildthryth arrived at Thoresburg, two men from the King's Guards were eating and drinking in a tavern. She told the king's men of the troll, and once they had finished eating and drinking, they rode swiftly to the King's Castle, where they told King Hereweald himself of the troll. King Hereweald ordered his guards to ride out, find this troll, and kill him.

The next day, the King's Guards rode forth from the castle along the King's Road. They found the stone hut by the roadside that the farmer's wife had told them about.

'Hello there!' one man called out as they approached the round hut.

'Hello my good friends', the troll said calmly.

'We are looking for a troll who is said to live around here. He calls himself "The Dragon-Slayer of Wessex". Is this your name?' the man asked.

'It is not my name. I have never heard it before.' the troll said.

'What is your name?' the man asked.

'My name is The Wizard of Wintanceaster.'

'That is no troll-name!' the man shouted. 'What is your real name?'

'That is indeed my real name. That is how I am known throughout the kingdom. Mention my name to any merchant of remedies or any wise man in the land, and he shall know that "The Wizard of Wintanceaster" means me.'

'Very well', said the man. 'If you should hear anything of this troll who calls himself "The Dragon-Slayer of Wessex", then tell us.'

'I shall', said the troll. 'Farewell.'

And the King's Guards rode on. They found many other trolls along the King's Road, though none with the name of 'The Dragon-Slayer of Wessex'.

A few weeks later, a young thane rode along the King's Road. He wore gold chains around his neck and a white ermine cloak. His face was lead-white and the dark brown locks of his hair were held back by a red band.

As the young thane and his men at arms cantered past the troll's hut, the troll shouted 'EEEUUUGGGHHH!!!'

'Who said that?' the young thane called out. 'Who's there?'

'Are you a boy or a girl?' the troll shouted.

'I am Delwyn, Thane of Holenmere. Who would dare speak to me in this way?'

'You look like a girl, but you talk like a boy. Are you a boy who wants to be a girl? That's disgusting. Are you trying to trick men into fucking you? That won't work. Your men at arms look like girls too.'

'You must be a troll.'

'No, I'm a talking fucking trout – of course I'm a troll! Now get off the King's Road! Go into the fucking woods so that no other younger, more impressionable boys see you.'

The Thane of Holenmere, who was unyielding even at twelve years old, nodded to his two men at arms. They dismounted, drew their swords, and strode over to the stone hut.

'You are foolish to think you can break through my walls!' the troll shouted.

The two guards crept around the stone hut, but found no way in, so they tried pulling the stones out of the wall with their hands.

'That'll take you a long time!' the troll said.

So instead the men at arms tried jabbing at the troll with their swords through the narrow gap through which the troll shouted at passers-by, but the swords were not long enough.

'Just as I thought – your men at arms are not so skilled with these swords.' the troll said.

'Either stop talking', the thane said, 'or leave this roadside.'

'I shall not leave this roadside! This is where I live!'

'Then stop talking.'

'Or what?!'

'Or I shall inform the king of your presence here, and he will send an army to smash down your walls and draw your intestines from the Sabrin to the Tames.'

'If you want me to stop talking, cut your cock off and shove it up your arse! Or give me your gold chain! I would even take that red band in your hair – a small price for my valuable time.'

'An army it is. What is your name, fetid troll?'

'My name is Osmund the Just.'

'That is no troll-name!' the thane shouted. 'What is your real name?'

'That is indeed my real name. That is how I am known throughout the kingdom. Mention my name to any fair and honest man in the land, and he shall know that "Osmund the Just" means me.'

'I am not a fool.' the thane said. 'I know that is not your real name. But it matters not. King Hereweald is a friend of mine, and I shall tell him personally that you squat in this hut by the roadside, and he shall send an army to smash your walls down, and kill you.'

And the Thane of Holenmere rode on, with his two men at arms behind him. They rode hastily to the King's Castle, where the young thane greeted King Hereweald and told him of the troll. Furious that a troll would speak to a thane at all (and furious at the increased number of problem trolls at the moment), King Hereweald sent half of all his men to travel along the King's Road and find this troll who called himself 'Osmund the Just'.

The king's men found the stone hut that the Thane of Holenmere had told them about, and they approached it, spears and shields raised.

'Hello my good friends', the troll in the hut said, calmly and pleasantly.

'We are looking for a troll who is said to live near here', the oldest and most battle-worn swordsman said. 'He calls himself "Osmund the Just". Is this your name?'

'It is not my name. I have never heard it before.' the troll said.

'What is your name?' the old man asked.

'My name is Wilfrith the Benevolent.'

'That is no troll-name!' the old man said. 'What is your real name?'

'That is indeed my real name. That is how I am known throughout the kingdom. Mention my name to any saint or righteous man in the land, and he shall know that "Wilfrith the Benevolent" means me.'

'Very well', said the old man. 'If you should hear anything of this troll who calls himself "Osmund the Just", then tell us.'

'I shall', said the troll. 'Farewell.'

And once again the king's men rode on. Together they could have torn down the troll's walls, and killed him, but they were tricked by the troll. They found many other trolls along the road, but they did not find a troll with the name 'Osmund the Just'.

A few more weeks later, and a young girl named Hilda was walking along the King's Road past the troll's hut. She was the daughter of Mildthryth, and her mother had told her all about the troll in the hut.

Hilda had always been quick-witted. She could read, she could write – she had a gift for mathematics, which she used to win bets with merchants who passed through Thoresburg. She was most knowledgeable of medicines too, and taught many others on the subject over the years after this story.

'EEEUUUGGGHHH!!!' said the troll in the hut as Hilda walked past.

Hilda said nothing, but looked in the direction of the hut, where the noise had come from. She recognised the hut – a round stone hut with tall walls and no door – it was just as her mother had described. This was where that fetid troll lived.

There was silence while the troll waited for Hilda to reply, but she did not.

'You're disGUSting!' the troll shouted. 'If you want to be pretty, try throwing up some of all the food you eat. If not, you might as well cut your arms with knives and die.'

'I know you', Hilda said. 'You're that troll who shouts things at people walking along the road.'

'I am indeed a troll. And I say what I like to people who walk by my castle.'

'What is your name?' Hilda asked.

'My name is Hrothgar the Valiant.'

'No it isn't.' Hilda said.

'What?!' the troll snorted.

'That's not your name – you made it up.'

'NO I DIDN'T! That is my name! Mention my name to any daring and fearless man in the land and 'e shall say that "Hrothgar the-'

'A few weeks ago you said your name was "The Dragon-Slayer of Wessex".' Hilda said. Her mother had told her all about the troll. 'And then you said your name was "The Wizard of Wintanceaster".' Hilda was a chatty person, and had been talking to the King's Guards when they had first come up the road looking for the troll.

'THOSE ARE DIFFERENT TROLLS!'

'But there's no way in or out of your hut.' Hilda said. 'You're the only troll who's ever been in there. You just keep making up new names to pretend that you've never said anything to the people walking along the road.'

'Are you a complete fucking idiot?! My name is Hrothgar the Valiant, I tell you!'

'No it isn't. What's your real name?'

'That is my real name! You stupid, ugly girl!'

But Hilda knew it was not. She continued walking down the road as the troll continued calling her 'fat' and 'ugly' and 'not pretty enough for him'.

'I will kill you stupid girl!' the troll shouted just before Hilda was too far away.

Curious what the troll's name really was, when she arrived at the town of Haeselford, where she had been heading before she met the troll, she went into the town's tavern. There she asked all of the townsfolk about the trolls they had encountered recently.

Many told the tale that they had heard from the men of the king's army, who had stopped there a few weeks before. They told of how they were looking for a troll who lived in a stone hut with the name 'Osmund the Just', but only found a troll with the name 'Wilfrith the Benevolent'. Clearly it was the same troll as 'The Dragon-Slayer of Wessex' and 'The Wizard of Wintanceaster'.

The townsfolk told of trolls with other names too. Each had met a troll with a different name: 'Eadric Lionstooth', 'Cynemaer Nine-eyes', 'Wilmaer Blackclaw', 'Wilmaer the Dragon-Slayer', 'Sigeberht, Thane of Odenesburg'. All, Hilda realised, were names of the same troll in the stone hut.

But what was the troll's real name? None of these false names were troll-names – none was his real name.

So Hilda continued on to the next town, a few miles further along the King's Road, and asked the folk in the tavern there. They too told of many trolls, each with a different name, but all living in an impenetrable hut by the King's Road.

But still no-one there knew the troll's real name, so Hilda continued on to the next town, and the next. When she visited the fifth town, she talked to the many men and women in the tavern there, and asked them if any of them knew the troll's real name.

'I don't know the troll's real name', a blacksmith said, 'but I know of someone who does. There is an old hag who lives in a hovel at the edge of a forest a mile north from here. She was friends with the troll when he lived under a bridge near here a few years ago. Go to her, and ask of the troll's name – she may tell you, but I warn you, you may find her unco-operative.'

So Hilda walked north to the edge of the forest, and found the hovel where the hag lived. It was squat, with a thatched roof and black smoke rising from a stone chimney.

'Hello?' Hilda called out.

There were clangs as metal pots hit the stone floor, hisses as potions hit flames, and an 'Ow!' from the hag inside. There were more clangs as the hag pushed her way to the oak door to the hovel and opened it.

'Who is it?! What do you want?!'

'My name is Hilda. I am from Thoresburg. I would like to ask you a question about a troll.'

'You want to move to Thoresburg?' the hag asked. She seemed preoccupied.

'No, I am *from* Thoresburg.' Hilda said. 'I want to ask you about a troll.'

'You want to ask a question about Thoresburg? You know you could just go there and see it for yourself.' the hag said.

'No.' Hilda said. The hag was most annoying. 'Listen to what I am saying! I want to ask you a question about a troll you know.'

'Oh I see,' the hag said. 'Go on then, ask it.'

'Well', Hilda began, 'there is a troll who lives in a stone hut by the side of the King's Road. He makes demands of those travelling along the road. The king's men keep coming to fight the troll, but he always gives a different name, so they never find him. He's called himself "The Dragon-Slayer of Wessex", "The Wizard of Wintanceaster", "Osmund the Just", "Wilfrith"-'

'Yes I know the troll you mean!' the hag said. 'What of him?'

'Do you know his real name?' Hilda asked.

'Yes I do.' the hag said.

'What is it?'

'Why should I tell you?' the hag said.

'Because he is using pretend names to avoid the King's Guards.'

'Well has he done anything unlawful?'

'He said he would kill me.'

'But that is not unlawful! He simply said some words! Now you are saying that he should be killed by the King's Guards for saying some words that you didn't like! No, I will not tell you his name, just so that you can take revenge on someone who said something you didn't like.' the hag said.

'He is a troll. I have not seen him, but most trolls are eight foot tall and stronger than an ox. If he wanted he could smash down his walls and kill me any time I am walking down the road. Why should I not believe him if he says he will kill me?' Hilda said.

'If a troll is actually attacking someone, then that is a problem for the king and the King's Guards to sort out. He is just saying words. You may not like them, but I see no reason to tell you his name so that you can tell the king's men and see the troll driven away.'

The blacksmith had been right. The hag was uncooperative. Hilda thought for a moment.

'If you don't tell me what the troll's name is', she said, 'I'll tell the King's Guards that you are friends with a troll, and you are helping him.'

'You dare threaten me, little girl!' the hag screeched. 'I may be old and live in a small hovel, but I am powerful. The sword or lance of a king's man is useless against my spells!'

'Perhaps you can defeat one man, but can you defeat a whole army? The king sent half of all his men out to defeat this troll. If he learns that you are protecting the troll, that army will come for you.'

The hag was silent while she thought.

'Very well', the hag said, 'I will tell you the name of the troll, as long as you agree that you will not tell the king's men to come for me.'

'Agreed.' Hilda said.

'His name is Gogog.' the hag said.

'And what does he look like?'

'He has green eyes – bright like emeralds – and a long scar down his right arm where a sword cut it.' the hag said. 'Now go! Leave me to my work. And remember our agreement, little girl!'

The witch went back into her hovel. Hilda walked back the way she had come. Blue sparkles and indigo steam shot out of the windows of the hovel behind her as the hag continued her work.

And so Hilda walked back along the King's Road until she arrived at the hut where the troll lived once again.

'EEEUUUGGGHHH!!!' the troll shouted through the gap in the stone wall. 'It's that stupid, fat little girl!'

'Oh hello', Hilda said. 'You're that troll who's called ... what was your name again?'

'My name is The Dragon-Slayer of Wessex.'

'That's not what you said last time.'

'What? Er ... er ...' the troll stumbled. 'The Wizard of Wintanceaster?' he asked.

'That's not what you said either.'

'Yes it is. That's my name.'

'You said "Osmund the Just".'

'Ah, well done little girl – you have passed my test. That is indeed my real name.'

'But you have not passed my test. That was not the name you gave me last time. Last time you said your name was "Hrothgar the Valiant".'

'No I didn't!'

'Yes you did.'

'You are making things up, you stupid, fat little girl.'

'Actually no, *you* are making things up.' Hilda said. 'You've made up all of these names, as well as others. But it doesn't matter – I know your real name. Your real name is Gogog.'

'What?! How did you know th- I mean ... That is not my name. I have never heard that name before in my life.'

'I found it out.' Hilda said, now knowing that she was right. 'I went and asked the hag that you are friends with, and she told me.'

'That stupid witch!' Gogog said bitterly.

'She also told me what you look like.' Hilda said. 'You have emerald-green eyes and a long scar down your right arm.'

The troll said nothing.

'Now if you don't leave this roadside and go and live somewhere else, and if you don't stop threatening those who walk along the road, I will tell the King's Guards what your name is and what you look like. And I will tell them that you pretend your name is different to what it actually is. They will come and find you; they will smash your walls down; they will recognise you; and they will kill you.'

'I will not leave!' Gogog said. 'And I will not be silenced! I provide valuable criticism of King Hereweald and his policies! If I cannot be allowed to say what I want, then you are letting King Hereweald do as he likes. That is why I must pretend that my name is something different to what it actually is. If the King's Guards knew my real name, they would easily find me and kill me for my views on the king, which the king does not like. I must invent names to avoid persecution!'

'You've never said *anything* about King Hereweald', Hilda said, 'or his policies. You don't invent names to *avoid* persecution – you invent names *in order to* persecute those who walk along the road.'

'IT IS MY RIGHT TO GIVE WHATEVER NAME I CHOOSE TO WHOMEVER I CHOOSE!' the troll in the hut shouted. 'AND IT IS MY RIGHT TO SAY WHAT I LIKE!'

'Then I shall tell the King's Guards your real name and what you look like.'

And Hilda walked away again, along the King's Road, while Gogog the troll called her 'arrogant' and 'patronising' and 'stupid', and threatened to kill her once again.

When Hilda arrived at Thoresburg, she found two of the king's men at the tavern. She told them of Gogog, and how he was the troll who called himself 'The Dragon-Slayer of Wessex', 'The Wizard of Wintanceaster', and all of the other names he had used. And she told them what he looked like.

The king's men rode for the King's Castle that afternoon, and told the king what Hilda had told them. The king once again ordered half his men to go and defeat this troll.

The king's army rode out to beyond Thoresburg, to Gogog's hut. Gogog once again tried to deceive the King's Guards with invented names, but they were not fooled. He would not – and indeed, could not – come out of his stone hut, so the king's men tore it down, stone by stone.

And when at last there was a gap in the wall that was large enough, and Gogog couldn't escape, the king's finest lanceman threw a spear through the gap in the wall, which went straight through Gogog's stomachs. A swordsman strode up to the impaled troll, and with a single swing of his sword, cut the troll's head off.

And that was the end of Gogog the troll.

# FLUNCG
# THE INDIGNANT

There was once a troll, whose name was Fluncg. Fluncg was apparently a female troll. My friend Baeda the Venerable believes that female trolls do not exist, and that only males exist. However, all accounts of Fluncg seem to agree that the troll was female. I'm not sure how they knew this – female trolls are said to be indistinguishable from male trolls. They are the same height; they are equally as fat; they are equally as strong; their voices don't sound any different. Some have reckoned that the trolls themselves can tell whether any other troll is male or female, but at the same time, trolls are almost never known to meet each other, so I don't think it really matters.

## On The Subject Of Trolls

Unlike most trolls, Fluncg did not live under a stone bridge or in a mud hut deep in a shadowy forest. (Many trolls dislike sunlight – some accounts even claim that trolls are turned to stone when struck by the sun's rays.) Fluncg lived out in the open. She lived in a meadow of foxgloves and daisies by the side of a road.

Of course, the reason why many trolls *do* live under bridges is because it's less dangerous. Any swordsman or bowman who saw them by the road might slay them if they were out in the open, so they hide under stone. But Fluncg seemed to be fine squatting in the mud by the roadside. Fluncg was said to be unusually tall for a troll – more than nine feet tall! Perhaps men at arms travelling along the road didn't fancy their chances. Though accounts also suggest that Fluncg was not particularly strong for her height.

Fluncg was not a particularly inconvenient troll most of the time. She sat by the roadside, on a mountain of her own shit, smashing turnips with a rock to make a kind of paste. She didn't threaten people on the road into giving her ham or chicken or bread. Most trolls like gold, but Fluncg didn't seem to be interested in the stuff. She did like fragrances, like Throch, which she sometimes asked for, but the main thing she asked for of travellers along the road was – amazingly – beetroot. She used it to stain the grey skin of her head bright red. No-one knows why she did that.

The mistake that most travellers made when passing Fluncg on the road was interacting with her at all. If you just carried on by, most of the time she took little interest in you.

One summer's day, Lady Sabrina was travelling along the road by which Fluncg sat. She travelled by horse-drawn carriage, and liked to look out through the window of it as she was carried across the countryside. As she saw Fluncg, sitting on a brown pâté, she said 'Great Oden, how disgusting.'

She said it very quietly, but unfortunately Fluncg was another troll with excellent hearing.

Fluncg looked up, her flabby neck wobbling. 'Um ... !!!' she said demandingly. 'What did you say?!'

Lady Sabrina was always strong-minded. I met her a few years ago on her seventieth birthday. She had no men at arms with her when she met this troll, and the carriage provided little protection, but she still said 'I said "how disgusting".'

'How dare you!' Fluncg snorted. 'That is most offensive! I can't believe that there is anyone in the land who would say that!' How dare you judge someone just because they have red hair!'

Lady Sabrina was perplexed by this. 'You don't have any hair.' she replied.

Fluncg's face went as red as the chunks of beetroot stuck to her bald head. 'That is MOST offensive! You can't say that! I have beautiful red hair, and people like you don't get to say otherwise!' she warbled.

'What are you talking about?' Lady Sabrina said, even more confused. 'You don't have any hair at all! You've just got beetroot stuck to your head! But it doesn't matter anyway – that's not why you're disgusting. You're disgusting because you are sitting on a mountain of your own shit!' Lady Sabrina shouted.

'YOU HAVE NO RIGHT TO SAY THAT!!!' the troll shouted. 'I AM BEAUTIFUL, AND PEOPLE LIKE YOU DON'T GET TO SAY OTHERWISE! YOU ARE AN ARROGANT, SPITEFUL, UGLY WOMAN!'

'I *do* have a right to say that.' Lady Sabrina said firmly. 'And you are deluded if you think it's not true.'

'HOW DARE YOU!' Fluncg spewed. 'HOW DARE YOU SAY THAT I MAY NOT SAY WHAT I WANT!'

'I didn't say that you deluded, unintelligent, shit-stained clump of pig fat!' Lady Sabrina said. Having had enough of the troll, she told her guardsman to keep going, leaving the troll to squat by the roadside.

'UM ... !!! WHERE DO YOU THINK YOU'RE GOING?!' Fluncg spat, sliding down her hill of shit and lolloping onto the road. 'YOU THINK YOU CAN JUST HARASS PEOPLE ON THE ROAD AND GET AWAY WITH IT?!'

'I have no interest in talking to you.' Lady Sabrina said. 'You are obviously deluded.'

'OH SO YOU DON'T THINK I HAVE THE RIGHT TO SAY WHAT I WANT?! YOU'RE TRYING TO TELL ME WHAT I CAN AND CAN'T SAY?!' Fluncg shouted at the carriage.

'No! That isn't what I said. Nor is it the same as what I said.' Lady Sabrina said impatiently.

'YOU ARE AN INTOLERANT WOMAN! I THINK YOU JUST DON'T WANT YOUR IDEAS TO BE CHALLENGED! YOU'RE A VERY ARROGANT, SPITEFUL, UGLY WOMAN!'

Fluncg squawked in outrage as she plodded behind the carriage. Lady Sabrina tried to ignore the troll.

The troll followed them for miles. In the evening, as the sun was setting, Lady Sabrina and her guardsman arrived at an inn. Fluncg was still behind them.

By this point Lady Sabrina had had quite enough of the troll, but there were no King's Men nearby to kill it, so she had to just ignore it. Lady Sabrina stepped out of her carriage, and walked to the front door of the inn. The innkeeper greeted her, and showed her to her room.

Fluncg trudged along a moment later, still tweeting about how offensive Lady Sabrina was.

'Stay back, foul troll!' Lady Sabrina's guardsman said, drawing his sword. Lady Sabrina's guardsman was an able fighter, but no match for the troll on his own. Thus he stood between the troll and the inn, but did not try to kill the troll.

Fluncg did not try to push past the guardsman either.

'Oh, well, I wonder if the owners of this inn know what you're *really* like!' Fluncg hooted towards the inn door. 'Innkeeper, innkeeper! Did you know that this woman attacked me while I was sitting by the roadside, just because I have red hair! She is an arrogant, spiteful, ugly woman, and I imagine you don't want anyone like *that* staying in your inn. You should chuck her out and force her to sleep in a ditch where she belongs!'

The innkeeper, who was an elderly man with long grey hair and who had known Lady Sabrina for years, stepped out through the doorway of his inn.

'Go away, foul troll', he said, 'or I shall ask for the king to have his men come and kill you!'

'*I* am not harming anyone.' Fluncg said proudly. 'I'm just standing here saying what I think.'

'I don't care what you think.' the innkeeper said.

'But do you care about what kind of person is staying in your inn?' the troll said smugly. 'You don't want people like Lady Sabrina staying in your inn.' Fluncg continued patronisingly. 'You don't want people to think that this inn is somewhere that *intolerant* people stay.'

'I don't care if you think Lady Sabrina is intolerant.' the innkeeper replied.

'Well fine, maybe you don't.' Fluncg screeched. 'Maybe you don't care if people are *intolerant*. Maybe you're quite an *intolerant* man yourself. Maybe you want everyone to think that this is where intolerant men stay, because you like being intolerant yourself. But did you know that Lady Sabrina hates Britons? I'm sure you don't want this inn to be known as a place where people like *that* stay. This inn is a fine place – you shouldn't have people like *her* staying in it.'

The innkeeper said incredulously 'Lady Sabrina does not hate Britons.'

'She does.' Fluncg chittered. 'She judges people based on how they look. She hates people with red hair; many Britons have red hair. Clearly she wants to rid the land of them. Is that really the kind of person you want staying in your inn? I don't think it is. Or if it is, then clearly you hate Britons too, and the king should send his men to take your gold and your inn and give them to someone who isn't *intolerant*.'

The innkeeper thought the troll quite ridiculous. He had known Lady Sabrina for almost two decades, and he knew that everything the troll said was nonsense. The troll was making it all up, though Fluncg seemed quite convinced of it herself. But did the troll really think that he would believe her over Lady Sabrina? Even if the innkeeper had never met Lady Sabrina before, Fluncg was a troll, so the innkeeper would *still* have believed Lady Sabrina over the troll. Did the troll really think that anyone would believe her?

Realising the futility of talking to the troll any longer, the innkeeper went back inside. Fluncg continued shouting at the door to the inn, but did not try to enter.

Lady Sabrina's guardsman stayed between the troll and the door. The troll continued shouting at the door throughout the night. Many times guests at the inn leant out of windows and told the troll to shut up or go away. Every time they did, Fluncg would try to convince them too that Lady Sabrina was an intolerant woman, who had attacked her on the road and who hated Britons. The troll tried to convince them that because the innkeeper had allowed Lady Sabrina to stay in the inn, the innkeeper too was intolerant. The innkeeper too liked to attack people on the road and wanted to rid the land of Britons. Unless the people staying in the inn wanted to become known as people who supported intolerant people, they should take the innkeeper's gold and his inn and chuck both him and

Lady Sabrina out and force them to sleep in a ditch, where worthless people like them belonged. None of the guests believed it – of course they didn't. Many people knew Lady Sabrina, and many people liked her. Did the troll really think that they would believe her over Lady Sabrina? Even if they had never met Lady Sabrina before, Fluncg was a troll, so they would *still* have believed Lady Sabrina over the troll.

Those staying in the inn did not sleep much that night. Only a few minutes before dawn did the troll stop shouting. When they looked out of their windows to see why, they saw that the troll was gone.

'Thank goodness', said the innkeeper as he walked out of the front door to the inn. 'If she had stayed here more than one night, she might have put people off staying in my inn.' he said to the guardsman.

'She went into the town a few minutes ago.' the guardsman said. 'She may yet come back.'

Fluncg had waddled into the middle of the town. It was a market town, and people were already hauling carts into the square to sell their produce. The sky was a faint pastel blue and there were no clouds to be seen. The air was cool in the early morning, but it would be a hot day.

'Attention everyone!' Fluncg yelled when she entered the market square.

The reaction of most was to run and hide behind carts or barrels. Some drew knives or blunt swords, but none were skilled fighters. The best they could hope for was that the troll didn't take *everything*.

But Fluncg wasn't interested in the bread and the honey that was being sold in the market square.

'The inn on the east road is where thieves and murderers stay! Everyone who is staying there is either a thief or a murderer!'

The people around the square were bemused by this. It obviously wasn't true. They all knew the old man who owned the inn. They knew that no such people stayed at that inn. What did the troll expect them to say?

'What are you talking about?' a blacksmith said. 'No they're not.'

'Well, maybe you're a thief and a murderer too? Maybe that's why you're so quick to defend them? You should be chucked out of this town, along with the other thieves and murderers in the inn on the east road. You should be forced to sleep in pig shit – that's what people like you deserve. I'm sure the *good* people of this town don't want it to become known as a town where people like you live.' Fluncg proclaimed hautily.

'Go away, foul troll', a carpenter said, 'or we shall ask for the king to have his men come here and kill you!'

'*I* am not harming anyone.' Fluncg said proudly. '*I'm* just standing here saying what I think.'

'We don't care what you think.' the carpenter said.

'Well perhaps you should.' Fluncg said with a face like a raspberry tart that had been kicked by a horse.

The townsfolk were utterly bewildered by this troll. They didn't understand what this troll wanted. Normally trolls wanted food and gold. While it was inconvenient to give trolls food and gold, if you gave it to them they at least went away for a while. But Fluncg didn't appear to want any of that. She didn't appear to want anything other than for everyone to believe her and for everyone to do what she said, despite the obvious fact that no-one at all in the market square had any interest in doing what Fluncg said.

Who knows what Fluncg might have done next were it not for Lady Sabrina? You see, Lady Sabrina had been thinking about the troll overnight (and listening to the troll too, for she had not slept for the troll's shouting). As she had thought and listened, she had understood what Fluncg was trying to do and how she was trying to do it. Lady Sabrina was always witty, and she had figured out how to defeat this particular troll without sword or the King's Men.

Lady Sabrina, holding two great legs of pork in her arms, waddled into the town square with the same gait as

Fluncg. She heaved and breathed arduously in the manner that trolls do, and let her mouth hang open in vacant stupidity.

'Look!' said Fluncg as Lady Sabrina plodded slowly into the square. 'See how so-called "Lady" Sabrina has stolen these two legs of pork from someone at the inn – doubtless some weary traveller on the road who did not suspect that this town was full of thieves!'

'Um ... !!!' Lady Sabrina said condescendingly. 'What did you say?'

Fluncg, who was too stupid to realise what Lady Sabrina was doing, said 'I said "See how so-called 'Lady' Sabrina has stolen these two le-'

'How dare you!' Lady Sabrina snorted. 'That is most offensive! I can't believe that there is anyone in the land who would say that! How dare you judge someone just because they are a man!'

Fluncg was perplexed by this. 'But you're not a man.' she dribbled.

Lady Sabrina puffed herself up and bulged out her eyes. 'That is MOST offensive! You can't say that! I am a gallant and noble man who has slain twelve dragons already this morning with my famous swords, and people like you don't get to say otherwise!' she warbled.

'You are clearly a woman!' Fluncg retorted. 'You are not a man! You are a mean, nasty, UGLY WOMAN!'

'YOU HAVE NO RIGHT TO SAY THAT!!!' Lady Sabrina shouted. 'I AM A VALIANT AND HANDSOME MAN, AND PEOPLE LIKE YOU DON'T GET TO SAY OTHERWISE! YOU ARE AN ARROGANT, SPITEFUL, DISGUSTING TROLL!'

'I HAVE THE RIGHT TO SAY WHAT I LIKE!' Fluncg shouted back. 'YOU ARE AN UGLY WOMAN!'

'HOW DARE YOU! I AM AN UGLY *MAN*!'

The townsfolk began to realise what Lady Sabrina was doing.

'I am the king of the town well!' one man shouted. 'How dare you not bow down before your sovereign!' he said, striding up to the troll.

'I am Saint Benedict the Impatient!' one woman shouted. 'How dare you linger in the presence of one so holy for so long!' she said, ambling up to the troll.

'I want to marry my cat!' another man shouted. 'The fact that you have remained silent on this thus far in the conversation shows that you clearly hate all cats. We should chuck you out of this town, lest anyone think that this is a town of people who hate cats!'

And soon everyone joined in, each making up reasons why the troll had caused such great offence, and each building upon the reasons why the troll should be thrown out of the town or killed.

Overwhelmed by the number and irrationality of the accusations of offence, Fluncg stumbled backwards. The crowd pressed on in false outrage, and Fluncg stepped back again. Soon the troll was running from the town with heavy stomps.

Fluncg was defeated. The townsfolk were relieved – they had gotten rid of the troll without losing anything and without needing the King's Men. They were forever grateful to Lady Sabrina for figuring out how to do it. Lady Sabrina continued travelling along the same road for many years, and every time stopped at the same inn, and the townsfolk would hold a small feast in her honour.

No-one ever saw Fluncg again. She did not go back to her mountain of shit by the roadside. There are no accounts of her being slain. I suspect that she retreated into the woods, and avoided all interaction with men and women.

# HLUTHG THE FIRST

There was once a troll, whose name was Hluthg. Now while many trolls have *some* redeeming qualities – Throch was able to speak coherently, and Gogog was content with his life in a hut by the roadside – Hluthg had no redeeming qualities at all. There was truly nothing to like about Hluthg. He was fat; he was ugly; he stank of pig shit and ear wax and vomit; he had an insatiable greed for gold, precious stones, rich food, and power; he could neither read nor write; he didn't seem to have the ability to listen. But above all, he was stupid. No troll I have ever heard about or written about seems to have been as stupid as Hluthg. He was so unintelligent, he could barely string a fucking sentence together.

And yet of any troll, Hluthg probably caused the most damage to any kingdom. Even more remarkably, one could argue that it was through no deliberate or planned action of Hluthg that it happened. Hluthg did not have the ability to think ahead, or make decisions based on what was likely to happen. (In fact he may not have had the ability to make decisions at all.) No, it was the people of the kingdom that allowed – indeed, compelled – Hluthg to wreak the havoc that he did.

You see, this story happened in the Kingdom of Northumbria many years ago. Northumbria had had a long line of terrible and short-lived kings. It started with Mad King Hrothgar, who was the son of Hildraed III. Upon his coronation, Hrothgar immediately declared war on the kingdoms to the south and west of Northumbria.

The war escalated quickly. And then just two years into the war, Hrothgar was slain on the battlefield. Some say that it was one of his thanes who did it.

Hrothgar had two sons: Sigeweard and Sigeberht. Sigeweard was the oldest, and rightly should have inherited the throne from Hrothgar, but the younger and jealous Sigeberht wanted the throne for himself. He stabbed his older brother while he was sleeping, and took the crown. It was unfortunate – had Sigeweard become king, Northumbria might have avoided many problems over the following thirty years.

King Sigeberht VIII, who was not quite as mad as his father, realised that there was no point in continuing the war, and called for a truce. The war ended, and the Northumbrians returned home. But King Sigeberht was greedy. He quadrupled the taxes on the people of Northumbria. He spent the gold he acquired on castles for himself and the lords he was friends with. This did not go unnoticed by the people of Northumbria, who quickly resented their king.

Some say it is fortunate – or indeed, providence – that King Sigeberht VIII died only eight years after his reign began. He died of a fever, though some say it was poison.

Sigeberht had just one son and five daughters. His son, Cyneric, was thirteen years old when he died.

Cyneric became king, though much to the frustration of the lords of Northumbria. Some lords, who had not liked his father's and grandfather's reign, believed that Northumbria needed an older, wiser king to resolve the problems that the kingdom had faced over the last decade. Other lords – those who had been the personal friends of King Sigeberht VIII, and who had been given great castles at the public's expense, thought that Cyneric lacked the ruthlessness of his father.

Cyneric became king. He certainly did *appear* to lack the ruthlessness of his father – at least at first. But he was far more cunning than his father. Cyneric did not raise the taxes, but he did not lower them either. Cyneric was said to be a great speaker. When common folk came to him to ask for a reduction in taxes, he was skilled at giving seemingly good reasons for why the taxes had to be so high – to protect the kingdom from the others that bordered it, to protect the kingdom from trolls and dragons and witches. Many people believed it, though many saw through the words. Cyneric kept most of the money for himself, and again rewarded the lords who were friendly to him – his father had taught him well. Cyneric built no castles himself, but he made those he had stronger. Most of his wealth he hoarded.

King Cyneric II lasted longer than his predecessors – he reigned for fifteen years. But something about age made the common folk trust him less.

This is where Hluthg comes into the story. Hluthg was a well-known troll in the Kingdom of Northumbria long before this. He'd been doing what all trolls do – coercing road-goers into giving him food and gold. Hluthg always had a particular liking for gold above all else. He decorated the bridges he lived under and the caves he lived in with it. Indeed, some travellers even enjoyed meeting Hluthg, for the way that he decorated his dwellings.

Hluthg was not known for being particularly 'good' at being a troll. He extorted gold and pork and mutton from some travellers, but he was never particularly strong, even though he was eight foot tall, and many of the wealthier lords could have their men at arms fight the troll off.

Perhaps it was the wealth hoarded by King Cyneric that drew Hluthg to Cyneric's castle – perhaps he was drawn by the gold in the king's vaults. But he arrived in the lower town around Cyneric's castle one day, the skin of his arms a maroon red from blood and mud, and the skin of his thighs and around his eyes yellow-white with clumped fat.

When the king's men saw him, they charged at the troll with lances. Hluthg flopped down on the first one – stomachs first – squashing him flat beneath his armour. The second man's lance sliced along the side of Hluthg's arm, but the cut was not deep. The troll brushed aside the lance, and then slapped the second man repeatedly, and clumsily, until he was knocked unconscious.

The town was busy, and the townsfolk leapt back at the sight of the troll (though not one of them tried to help the king's men, for they resented the king's men as much as the king).

'I am going to kill King Cyneric!' Hluthg shouted.

And then Hluthg just stood there, gawping around, as though he had forgotten the thing he had just said.

The townsfolk didn't know what to make of this at first. They didn't like King Cyneric, but they didn't like trolls either.

'Good.' an old farmer said. 'I'll give you meat and bread if you get my tax money back after you kill him.'

'I will.' Hluthg said, and the old farmer took out some lamb and a loaf of bread from a leather bag at the front of his cart. He gave it to the troll, and Hluthg sat down at an oak table by the side of the street, and began eating.

A tanner's wife, who saw what the old farmer did, walked up to the troll.

'I will give you honey and water if you get *my* tax money back after you kill the king.' she said.

'I will.' Hluthg said, and he grabbed the honey and the jug of water that the tanner's wife offered him. He spread the honey over the remaining bread, and gulped down the water.

An innkeeper, who saw what the old farmer and the tanner's wife did, walked up to the troll.

'You may stay in the largest room in my inn overnight, if you also get *my* tax money back after you kill the king.' he said.

'I will.' Hluthg said, and once he had finished eating and drinking, he followed the innkeeper through the doors of his inn.

One of the king's men (who had not fought the troll) saw all of this happen. He ran up the hill to the king's castle, through the main gate, and into the king's court chamber, where King Cyneric was sitting at the head of a table, feasting with the reeves of the kingdom.

The king's man told the king what he had seen: that the troll had entered the town, that the troll had crushed two of the king's men, and that three townsfolk had offered the troll food, drink, and a room to kill the king and get their tax money back.

Since the troll was not causing a problem for the townsfolk, King Cyneric decided not to risk more of his men trying to fight off the troll. The townsfolk might fight off the troll themselves, once they realised how repugnant the troll was.

The king issued no decree, but Hluthg was allowed to stay in the town.

That evening, news of the troll spread quickly around the town. Half of the townsfolk were repulsed by the thought of a troll staying in the town. The other half, like the old farmer, the tanner's wife, and the innkeeper, saw the opportunity that the troll presented. If the troll really did kill the king, they would all get their tax money back. So they overlooked their disgust at the troll.

The next day, as the troll was shuffling through the streets of the town, looking for food, many more townsfolk came and asked that the troll return their tax money after killing the king. One man offered the troll a pair of fine leather boots, that he had made overnight specially for the troll (for trolls have far larger feet than men and women). Another man offered the troll a fine white ermine cloak that he had previously intended to sell to a wealthy lord. And a swordsmith offered the troll the finest weapon he had made that year: a greatsword with a ruby set into the pommel. He offered it to the troll so that the troll may use it as he killed the king.

As the troll shuffled around, brown sweat dripping down onto the stone of the streets, the same king's man from the day before followed him, and observed him. At the end of the day, he returned to the king once again, who was again sitting in the court chamber, eating glazed meats and fruits from far-away lands with his loyal lords.

Once again the king's man told the king of what he had seen, but King Cyneric was still not bothered by the troll.

'Whatever the people think of the troll now', the king said, 'soon they will find him disgusting. For he is a troll, and he is so obviously disgusting.'

That evening, news of the troll continued to spread, this time beyond the walls of the town, to the rest of the kingdom. Half of those who heard of Hluthg were repulsed by the thought of a troll wandering freely through the town. The other half saw the opportunity that the troll presented. If the troll really did kill the king, they would all get their tax money back. So they overlooked their disgust at the troll.

The next day, many of those in the kingdom who had heard of the troll, and realised what the troll could do for them, travelled to the town around the king's castle. They each carried with them something precious or valuable to give to the troll. Some brought food and drink; others brought silver, gold, or rubies; others brought helmets, shields, and maces.

The people of the kingdom lined up to give their gifts to the troll, as the troll sat outside the inn, eating meat and shitting into a wooden bucket, which was promptly emptied by those now loyal to the troll.

Those in the kingdom who had remained disgusted by the troll stayed at home.

Once again, the king's man who had spied on the troll the previous day, spied on the troll throughout this day. In the evening, he again returned to the king and told him what he saw.

'I am surprised that the common folk have tolerated the troll for this long.' the king said. 'But soon they will realise how disgusting he is, and turn against him. Still, should he try to come within a hundred yards of the castle, kill him.'

The next morning, thousands of common folk had filled the town, and stood outside the great house that the troll now lived in. When the troll awoke, he stepped out of his front door, carrying the greatsword he had been gifted (though none of the armour).

Upon seeing the troll, the crowd roared. They chanted 'Death to Cyneric! Death to Cyneric! Death to Cyneric!'

Hluthg gawped at them all. He may have forgotten that he had sworn to kill the king, but the crowd compelled him onward.

Hluthg plodded forward, up the street, towards the king's castle. The crowd swarmed around him.

A line of king's men stood at one hundred yards away from the gates of the castle. They saw the troll and the crowd approaching. They drew their swords, lowered their lances, and nocked their arrows.

But seeing the king's men, the crowd surged forwards, ahead of the troll. They outnumbered the king's men a thousand to one. They had no weapons or armour, but the king's men did not expect to have to fight them. So within moments, the crowd had pushed through the line of lances, and pushed down the king's men into the mud of the road. They stole their swords and stabbed them through the neck, or stole their shields and bashed them against the ground. A few common folk were injured, but the injuries were minor, and all of the first line of king's men were dead. Hluthg, who was closer to the back of the crowd than the front, continued plodding forwards up the street, seemingly unaware of what the crowd was doing.

The crowd and Hluthg reached the gates of the castle, where another line of the king's men stood guarding them. They had not seen what had happened to their fellow guardsmen down the street, for there was a bend in the road. They too drew their swords, lowered their lances, and nocked their arrows.

Being warier of the crowd than the guards down the road, they loosed arrows and swung swords at the crowd sooner. A few of the common folk were slain, but not many, for they still outnumbered the guards a thousand to one. All of the guards were killed, and the common folk surged through the gates of the castle. Hluthg was at the back of the crowd.

The common folk smashed through the oak doors to the king's court. King Cyneric was, once again, enjoying a great feast with his lords in the shadow of his throne. Upon seeing the common folk burst through the doors, the guards who stood around the room reached for their swords. But the common folk overpowered them too quickly, and soon they were all dead too.

The common folk made no accommodation for the lords who sat around the great table. They pulled the lords from their seats, stabbed them, beheaded them, then dragged their bloody bodies across the smooth wooden floor, and hurled them from the window. When all but the king were dead, they grabbed the king, his face as white as ice, and pulled him up in front of his golden throne.

A few minutes later, Hluthg shuffled into the room, staining every surface he touched with the grease and shit that coated his small hands. The crowd stood around the edges of the throne room, watching the troll as he lolloped towards the restrained king.

With a heave and a fart, Hluthg lugged the bejewelled greatsword over his head and down on King Cyneric II. Because of the angle from which Hluthg had swung the sword, it cut down through part of Cyneric's head, neck, and shoulder. It did not fully behead him, but he certainly did die. The sword cut a short way into his golden crown, and when Hluthg pulled the sword away, the bloody crown was stuck to it.

The former king's body slumped to the floor as the crowd cheered. Hluthg wrenched the crown from the sword, and placed it on his own head. Cyneric's blood dripped down Hluthg's face, turning his clotted skin an even deeper shade of maroon. The troll kicked the king's body aside, and shuffled forwards to the throne. He plopped his flabby arse on the velvet seat, and stared forwards mindlessly.

The old farmer, who had been the first to support the troll's ambition, stepped forwards from the crowd.

'Long live King Hluthg the First!' he proclaimed.

Half the crowd cheered. The other half looked around in confusion. They had known that Hluthg was going to kill the king (although in truth, they hadn't needed Hluthg at any point), but they didn't know that the troll was going to become king in Cyneric's place.

'Long live King Hluthg the First!' half the crowd chanted. Hluthg continued to stare forwards, mouth open, eyes half-lidded.

'After a long day', Hluthg said as the midday sun shone through the windows, 'I shall retire, and tomorrow I shall begin and start the important work of ruling this noble, noble, very noble, really good kingdom.'

The crowd were confused for a moment. 'What about all our money?' one man said.

'This evening I shall begin counting the gold – the big gold, very big gold – that is in the vaults of this castle and tomorrow I shall distribute it back to you all.' King Hluthg said.

The common folk were quite satisfied with that, so they began to shuffle out of the throne room (though several took some of the silver plates and cutlery that lay around with them).

Hluthg pulled the great oak table at which the former king and his lords had been feasting closer to the throne, and then he continued the feast that they had not finished, eating honeyed pork and beef stew with dumplings and dates from the south.

The common folk went back to their business about the town and the kingdom. The tale of what had happened spread quickly, to every man, woman, lord, and king in the land. Those in Northumbria who had found the troll disgusting were shocked by it, and mortified that their kingdom was now ruled by a gruesome troll (though even they recognised the advantages of no longer having Cyneric on the throne).

The next day, many of the remaining reeves and thanes of Northumbria travelled to the king's castle. Some travelled there planning to slay this troll, and place upon the throne a man worthy of it – someone as legitimate as Cyneric but not as malicious. But others travelled for a different reason, for now that Hluthg sat on the throne, a new opportunity was presented to them.

The lords arrived at the king's castle. They walked into the throne room to find the troll asleep on the throne. Dried stew stained his mouth, and date stones were scattered across the floor. King Hluthg I had not bothered to find the privy, and had instead just shat in one of the bowls that a lord had been eating from the day before. The bowl was still on the table.

'The troll is asleep', Lord Osraed said. 'We should kill him now, before he wakes.' Lord Osraed's men began creeping forwards, drawing their swords.

'Troll!' Lord Eadric said, to wake the troll. The others looked around sharply in frustration.

Hluthg snorted awake. 'Who are you?!' he said upon seeing them.

'We are the lords of Northumbria, your majesty.' Lord Eadric said in oily tones. Lord Osraed's men sheathed their swords and stepped back. They could have overpowered Hluthg easily, as he was not strong, but most trolls are indeed very strong, and they assumed this of Hluthg too.

'What do you want?!' Hluthg belched.

'Well we are here to assist you, your majesty, in the affairs of the kingdom.' Lord Eadric replied. Half of the lords looked at Eadric with disgust; the other half played along.

You see Eadric and the other lords realised what they could do. Sure, one king was dead, and now a rancid troll wore the crown of Northumbria, but the common folk had chosen this troll to be their king. If they were willing to look past the troll's foul stench and the gunk that dripped from his flabby arms, what else would they ignore? The lords of Northumbria could raise taxes yet again, and hold back the best food for themselves. The troll was too stupid to know what was going on. As long as the troll didn't try to kill them – which, if he were given all of the meat and gold that he wanted, he wouldn't – they would be fine. Lord Eadric was, by all accounts of him, a bit of a shit.

Hluthg stared into the distance with his mouth open. 'Bring me honeyed milk and steak!' he spat.

Lord Eadric ordered some of his men to do so, and to find handmaidens from the town who would serve the troll.

Hluthg ate, drank, and shat his way through the remainder of the day, while Lord Eadric secured the castle vaults. Lord Osraed, and the other lords who despised the troll, returned home, for Lord Eadric was wealthy, and had many more men – were it to come to a battle, Lord Eadric would win.

By the end of the day, many of the common folk who had been promised gold by the troll returned to the castle, for they had been expecting to receive it that day, as the troll had said. Lord Eadric ensured that they were permitted into the throne room, where Hluthg sat, with the blood-stained crown on his head, so that they could speak to him directly.

'Your majesty', one farmer said, 'may we have the gold that you promised to return to us?'

'We are in the process – a great word "process" – of returning it to you. We are counting it; there's a lot of it; there are mountains and mountains of gold beneath this castle, I tell you. If I weren't giving it all away I would be very wealthy – I would be the wealthiest king in the land. But I'm not keeping it; I'm not giving it away; I'm giving it back to the people who took it from you, which is you.' Hluthg said, spitting chewed meat and egg across the table.

It didn't make sense, of course. The common folk were confused by what the troll was saying, but they understood generally what the troll meant – he was counting the money to give it back to them. It all seemed to make sense.

But of course, no such thing was happening. Lord Eadric had counted the money, sure, but he had counted it for his own books. And Hluthg, while he had promised anything at all to get himself inside the king's castle in the first place, even something as precious to him as gold, now that he was there, he rather fancied keeping the gold to himself and his new lordly friends.

For a few days, common folk kept returning to the castle, to ask their troll-king for the gold he promised them. But every day he said something incomprehensible, or simply didn't talk about it at all. The common folk left again, sure that everything was fine.

Those in the kingdom who had not elected to crown the troll king repeatedly asked those who had where their money was. They repeatedly told them that the troll was never going to give the gold back, because he was a troll, and that's what trolls do. But those who had fought for Hluthg insisted that even though they didn't have their tax money yet, it was better to have Hluthg on the throne than Cyneric – better a foul troll than a malicious man.

Days turned to weeks; weeks turned to months; and months turned to years. *Years!* For *years* Hluthg the First sat upon the throne of Northumbria! As time went on, everyone became sort of used to it. All of the kingdoms bordering Northumbria were astonished. Every day that went by they were astonished that Hluthg still lived.

In the weeks and months following Hluthg's coronation, Lord Eadric seized control of the castles and keeps held by those lords who had been in the throne room when Cyneric was killed. The land those lords had owned was given to many of the neighbouring lords –

those who were loyal to Eadric and to Hluthg. The taxes from those lands also went to those loyal lords. From the point of view of the common folk, it made no difference – they still paid taxes to someone – but now more land was owned by fewer people.

Lord Eadric was able to placate Hluthg with food and gold for several months (for the first month and a half, the troll never even left the throne room). But trolls are insatiably greedy. They are also often highly opinionated. Hluthg began to demand that new laws be enforced to his liking.

Much like Gogog, Hluthg didn't like 'pretty boys'. He demanded that it be outlawed for men to wear anything made of silk or velvet. They could not wear anything brightly coloured. And they were banned from wearing fragrances too. This only interfered with the lives of a few people – mostly sons of reeves and thanes – few of the common folk were affected or even interested.

Every day, those common folk who had always been disgusted by the troll told those who had fought for Hluthg that they would never get their tax money back. And still those who had fought for the troll insisted that they would, or that it didn't matter, or that they had even effectively gotten it back anyway, since they had avoided tax rises that there would have been under Cyneric (not that Cyneric ever raised taxes, as far as is accounted).

After a few years on the throne, Hluthg even outlawed any criticism of him – by noble or common folk alike. Those who dared to say anything against him were seized by Eadric's men and hanged or burned.

Traders from nearby kingdoms stopped coming to Northumbria. The money they might make stopped being worth the chance of something they said being mistaken for an insult against the troll-king.

Many people left Northumbria too. Northumbria was no longer a prosperous place. Taxes were so high, and wealth concentrated in the hands of so few, that farmers could not grow enough food to live while selling enough of it to pay the owner of the land. So they left. Many went to Mercia and Wessex.

After eight years, Northumbria was an impoverished kingdom. The people who remained had little money, and hardly enough food to live. Picts had begun raiding the northern lands of the kingdom. The troll-king had done nothing about it.

Hluthg had remained as indifferent to the common folk as ever, but he had demanded more and more from Lord Eadric. After eight years on the throne, Hluthg was twice as fat as at the start of his reign. He was so fat he could no longer actually sit on the throne. Instead he just sat on the stained floor in front of it. He ate nothing but the finest meat – he didn't even eat bread or sweet fruits anymore. Every day he demanded new clothes – expensive clothes made out of leather and ermine and velvet. He refused to wear anything that had been washed.

After eight years even Lord Eadric was fed up with the troll. I suppose he deserved it. Meeting the troll's demands was increasingly difficult and expensive. And the common folk no longer seemed interested in the troll. They had long since stopped coming to ask for their tax money back. Many of the common folk resented Hluthg as much as they had resented Cyneric, and the troll's former supporters were no longer interested.

Eight years to the day after Hluthg had killed King Cyneric II, Lord Eadric opened the doors to the throne room in the middle of the night when the troll was asleep. He took an arrow, nocked it in a bow, and aimed at the troll. He loosed it, and the arrow went straight through the troll's open mouth.

Hluthg was dead instantly, but Lord Eadric loosed two more arrows at the troll just to be sure. The troll hardly made a sound as he died.

Lord Eadric took the ruby greatsword that Hluthg had been given years before, and cut off Hluthg's head. With a small knife, he cut away the stained crown that had gotten stuck to the troll's head, and then chucked the head out of a high window. Lord Eadric washed the bloody crown, and the next morning, the kingdom woke under the reign of King Eadric I.

For most, the proclamation of the new king made little difference to their lives, just as it had been with kings before the troll-king.

Life in Northumbria improved during King Eadric's reign. The laws that Hluthg had implemented were gradually removed. Taxes were lowered again. Traders returned to Northumbria. But King Eadric only oversaw these changes because they were an advantage to himself. More trade meant more tax revenue, and more money for himself and his family. The fact that it improved life for everyone in Northumbria was not important.

Ultimately the people of Northumbria did not learn anything. Even once the troll was dead, those who had helped the troll to become king insisted that it had been the right thing to do, even though they had never gotten what they wanted.

Hluthg in the end got everything he wanted. Sure, he was killed by an arrow, but all trolls are killed eventually. Hluthg had eight years of fine food and fine clothes in one of the largest castles in the land before being killed. Hluthg was the wealthiest troll to ever live, and got to inflict his will on more people than any other troll to live before or since.

This whole story could have been avoided if Cyneric had had the troll killed when he first entered the town, as any wise king would have done. Or it could have been avoided if the people of Northumbria had remembered that Hluthg was a troll, and you should never believe the words of a troll. So if there is anything that can be learned from this story it is that a troll is a troll, and no matter what they say, a troll will always do what trolls do.

# Plolg
# the Common

I have written much about unusual trolls – trolls who have achieved things that we do not expect of such unintelligent creatures. But most trolls are not like this – most trolls are not cunning like Throch, deceptive like Gogog, or popular like Hluthg. Most trolls are just stupid. Let me tell you of a troll named Plolg.

This story happened only a few months ago, in spring, in the twentieth year of the reign of King Eadweard. A farmer from a town near to Oxford was walking along a road. He came to a bridge over the Tames.

Under this bridge squatted the troll Plolg. Upon seeing the farmer approach the bridge, the troll leapt out from under it, onto the stonework of the bridge, blocking the man's way.

'Gold!' Plolg grunted.

The farmer, whose name was Godwin, realised what the troll meant, and said 'I have no gold.'

'GOLD!' Plolg grunted again, lurching forward in greed.

'I don't have any gold!' Godwin shouted back.

Plolg just stared at the farmer, breathing through his open mouth, tongue hanging out. Watery snot slipped down his face. His legs were silty from standing in the deep river.

Either the troll had not heard or not understood – the farmer couldn't tell.

'I DON'T HAVE ANY GOLD!' the farmer shouted again.

The troll continued to stare dully, as he tried to understand what the farmer was saying.

After a minute, the troll said 'HAM!'

'I don't have any ham either.' Godwin said.

'HAM!' Plolg shouted again, stamping his fat foot on the mossy stone of the bridge, and shaking his tiny hands in protest.

'I. DON'T. HAVE. ANY. HAM!!!' the farmer said once again. Although trolls are very tall and very strong, and could easily crush a man with a single thigh, the most annoying thing about encounters with them is not their physical intimidation – it is exchanges such as these.

'BEEF?' asked Plolg.

'No.' Godwin replied.

'UUURRRGGGHHH!!!' Plolg shouted. He kicked the wall of the bridge, smashing several of the stones off it, tumbling into the river below. 'I WANT MUTTON!!!' Plolg said.

He swung at the farmer with a slimy hand. He struck the farmer's jaw, sending him flying backwards.

The farmer hit the ground several yards away. The stone of the bridge cut into his arms and hands as he landed.

Plolg was about to charge at the farmer and kill him, when from the woods on the far side of the bridge sounded a horn.

A moment later, a hundred armoured men with swords and lances rode out of the woods, followed by the king. It was fortunate for the farmer that the king happened to be riding to Oxford that day.

Upon hearing the horn, Plolg stopped still, his grey eyes wide looking upon the men riding towards the bridge.

The men halted as they rode onto the first stones of the bridge, and parted to allow the king through.

'What is happening here?' the king demanded to know.

'This troll is trying to steal from me.' Godwin said. 'When I did not give him gold or food, he attacked.'

'NO!' shouted Plolg. 'He struck me first!' the troll said. 'He is thief and criminal and violent!'

Now, I have been advising the king for many years on the subject of trolls. I have told him of all the trolls I have written about here, and many more.

The king did not need to hear anymore. It was obvious what had happened. It was the same thing that always happened. Why would anyone believe the troll? The troll had no cuts in his grey skin, whereas the farmer had many. The troll was standing; the farmer had been thrown to the ground. Though the king had not seen for himself what had happened, it was obvious.

The king asked for a lance from one of his men. Plolg realised what was going to happen, and turned, and ran across the bridge, trying to get away. Plolg could have just hopped off the side of the bridge and swum downstream, but trolls are stupid.

The king aimed his lance at the troll, and kicked his horse into a gallop. A moment later, the king drove his lance through Plolg's neck, killing the troll almost instantly.

The king's men pulled the lance from the troll's neck once it was dead, and then left the body to rot in the woods. They brought the farmer to the nearest town, and the king paid for the farmer's injuries to be stitched and bound, and the king, the farmer, and the king's men had a great feast to celebrate the death of Plolg.

And that is how one deals with trolls.

# A LIST OF WORDS USED IN OLD ENGLISH NAMES

**aelf**
'elf'

**aethele, aethel**
'noble'

**beorht**
'bright', 'clear'

**cyne**
'royal'

**ead**
'rich', 'wealthy'

**frith**
'peace'

**gar**
'spear'

**gifu**
'gift'

**god**
'good', 'god'

**here**
'army'

**hild**
    'warfare', 'combat'

**hroth**
    'fame'

**maer**
    'famous'

**mund**
    'protector', 'protection'

**os**
    'god'

**raed**
    'advice', 'wisdom', 'counsel'

**rice, ric**
    'strong', 'powerful', 'rich'

**sige**
    'victory', 'victorious'

**stan**
    'stone'

**thryth**
    'might', 'majesty'

**weald**
    'power', 'authority'

**weard**
    'guardian'

**wil**
    'will', 'desire'

**wine, win**
    'friend'

Printed in Great Britain
by Amazon